© Creation, script and illustrations: A.M. Lefèvre, M. Loiseaux,
M. Nathan-Deiller, A. Van Gool
First published and produced by
Creations for Children International,
Belgium • www.c4ci.com
© 2009 Peter Haddock Publishing, United Kingdom, YO16 6BT
www.phpublishing.co.uk
Printed in China

VAN GOOL

5 minute bedtime tales

Puss in Boots

One day, a poor peasant inherited a cat. "What can I do with you?" he said. "I haven't even got enough food to feed myself!" "Do not worry, master," replied Puss. "Give me some boots and a hat and I will make you a rich and happy man." Puss took his master to a stream. "Take off your clothes and dive into the water quickly,"

he said, and hid his old clothes. At that very moment, the king's carriage passed by. Puss called out, "Help! Help! My master, the Marquis of Carabas, is drowning!"

Immediately the king ordered the man to be saved and dressed him in fine silk clothes. Puss pointed to a nearby castle and said to the king, "To thank you, my master invites you to his palace." While his master was riding in the king's carriage, Puss ran to the castle.

7

like a young prince and the princess could look at nobody else. The two of them fell in love. When the king had eaten, he said to Puss's master, "My dear Marquis, you are a

It belonged to a wicked giant who ruled over the lands around it. "Sire," said Puss, "I have heard that although you are a giant, you can turn yourself into something as small as a mouse. This must surely be a joke?" The ogre was cross and immediately changed into a little mouse ... and Puss leapt on him and gobbled him up! The castle now belonged to the Marquis of Carabas! Puss arranged a delicious banquet for the king, his daughter, the princess, and all their servants. In his beautiful robes, Puss's master looked just

fine, rich man and my daughter likes you very much. You may have her hand in marriage." The Marquis accepted with delight. They were married without delay and the happy couple lived in the palace. And naturally Puss in Boots lived with them very happily ever after!

Goldilocks and the Three Bears

One morning, the three bears went for a walk, leaving their hot bowls of porridge on the table to cool down. But they forgot to lock the door.

At the same time, a little girl called Goldilocks set out for a walk in the forest. She got lost and grew very hungry. In a

clearing she saw a little cottage. "I'll ask for something to eat," she thought. She knocked at the door, but no-one answered. Goldilocks pushed open the door and saw the three bowls of porridge on the table. "Mmm, they look good," she said. She tried all the bowls.

She didn't hear the three bears come back. "Someone has eaten my porridge," cried Baby Bear. "And someone has broken

One was too hot and one was too cold but the porridge in the smallest, was best. "Delicious!" she said, and ate it all. Then she saw a little chair by the fireplace. She sat down, but the chair broke into pieces and she fell to the floor. "Bother," she said crossly. "I am so tired." She climbed the stairs to find a bed. One bed was too hard and one was too soft, but the smallest bed was just right.

my chair," he wailed. The three bears crept upstairs and found Goldilocks fast asleep in the small bed. When she opened her eyes there were the three bears looking at her. With a cry she ran away and never came back. And the three bears thought this was a very good thing!

The Bear and the Little Wrens

As the bear and his friend the wolf were walking through the forest one day, they heard a beautiful song. "Who is that?" asked the bear, enchanted. "That's the king of the birds, the wren," said the fox. The bear was determined to see this fine

disappointed by the little chicks he saw in the nest. "It is impossible that these

creature, but when he climbed the tree where the nest was, the king and queen wren had flown off. He was most

wretched little creatures are the children of a king," he said. The chicks were cross, and when their parents returned they said that they would eat nothing until the bear apologised for what he had said. The parents were also annoyed and went to the bear to demand an apology. The bear refused indignantly.

War was declared. The bear ordered all four-footed animals to join his army, and the wrens called on all flying creatures to

help them. Their cunning king sent a fly to spy on the animals' army. The fly hid under a leaf and listened. The bear appointed his officers, and the crafty fox was made general of the army. "These will be my signals," said the fox. "When I raise my bushy tail in the air, we will advance. If I pull it between my legs, run away as fast as you can." Next day the two armies faced each other. But the fly had done his work well, and the battle had hardly begun when the wren sent a bee to sting the fox's tail. At once the fox pulled his tail between his legs to protect it. When the other

animals saw this, they turned and ran away, as the fox had ordered. The birds had won! The bear apologised to the little chicks, who had a feast of worms to celebrate.

Little Red Riding Hood

Little Red Riding Hood set out to take a basket of cakes to her sick grandmother. "Go quickly," said her mother. "Don't speak to any strangers." But when Little Red Riding Hood saw the birds and the flowers on her way through the wood,

she forgot her mother's words. Suddenly a big grey wolf appeared. "Where are you going, little girl?" he asked politely. "I am going to visit my grandmother," she replied. The wolf was very pleased. He would have the girl and her grandmother for dinner! The cunning wolf pretended that he knew a quick way to the house and showed Little Red Riding Hood the path. Meanwhile, he ran across the wood and got to the grandmother's house first.

"All the better to smell you with," said the wolf. "And what big teeth you have," she said. "All the better to eat you with," roared the wolf, and gobbled her up. The wolf fell asleep and began snoring loudly. A hunter heard the noise and entered the house. He saw the wolf with

He knocked on the door. "It is Little Red Riding Hood!" he said, trying to sound like a child. The old lady called, "Come in, my dear." At once the wolf swallowed her up. Then he put on her nightdress, put on her bonnet and slipped into her bed. Soon afterwards, Little Red Riding Hood came in. "Grandmother, what big eyes you have!" she said in surprise. "All the better to see you with," said the wolf in a quavering voice. "What a big nose you have," said Little Red Riding Hood.

his swollen tummy and guessed what had happened. He hit the wolf so hard that it spat out the little girl and her grandmother. Red Riding Hood thanked the hunter. "From now on," she promised, "I will always listen to my mother!"

Bambi

All the animals and birds in the forest were very excited. A fawn, a baby deer,

had just been born. They hurried to see him. "He's lovely," they said. "What's his name?"

His mother smiled proudly. "I shall call him Bambi," she replied. Little Bambi soon learnt how to stand and walk, and his mother often took him to explore the fields. There were so many interesting things to discover. "What's this pretty flower at the end of my nose?" he asked.

Bambi was very surprised when a voice said, "I'm not a flower, I'm a butterfly!"

One day there were terrible crashes in the forest. "Quick!" cried a hare. "Run! It's the hunters!" Bambi ran and hid, but

when he returned home, his mother was not there. Bambi waited a very long time. At last he realised she would never come back. A few days later, it grew cold, and huge flakes of snow began to fall.

"What is this?" thought Bambi, for he had never seen snow

before. When he went to drink from the pond, the water was frozen solid. It was very slippery, and Bambi bumped into a pretty female fawn. "Hello Bambi," she said. "I'm your cousin, Faline." They became friends at once and set off to find something to eat. It was hard, because the grass was hidden under the snow. Bambi was happy. He would never be alone in the forest again, and spring was coming.

The Little Mermaid

There was once a little mermaid who lived in a palace deep under the sea. One day, she swam to the surface and saw a large boat; a handsome prince was on the deck. Suddenly, huge waves rocked the boat.

the mermaids. But, because she was ashamed of her fishy tail, she swam back

The prince fell into the sea, but he couldn't swim. The little mermaid swam down to the prince and carried him to the shore. To wake him up, she sang a magic song of

to the bottom of the sea before he opened his eyes. When the prince opened his eyes and looked around him, there was no-one else on the beach. The little mermaid couldn't forget the handsome prince. But to live on land she needed legs.

"I will help you," said the Sea Witch, "if you will give me your lovely voice." No sooner said than done! Suddenly the mermaid found herself standing on the beach. When she came to the palace the prince

was enchanted with her beauty and asked her to dance. But the little mermaid couldn't speak a word and after a while he left her to dance with others. Desperate, the mermaid went to the seashore to meet her sisters. Using signs, she asked them to beg the witch to return her voice. The Sea Witch told them, "I will return her voice, but in exchange I want your silky hair!" Because they loved their sister, the mermaids sacrificed their silky hair. The spell was lifted and the little mermaid began to sing. The prince recognised the song that had saved him from the sea. Filled with love, he asked the little mermaid to marry him. Now the little mermaid was a princess and lived happily ever after with her prince!

The Little Red Hen

The little red hen was walking through a field with her chicks one day when she found some grains of corn. She carried them back to the farmyard. "We should plant these," she said. "Who will help?" "Not me," said the pig, the duck and the cat all together. They got on with what they were doing while the little hen

planted the corn. A few weeks later the grains had grown tall and had fine ears of

wheat. "It is time to cut it," said the little red hen. "Who will help?" Like a chorus, the pig, the duck and the cat said, "Not me." They got on with what they were

doing while the little hen cut the corn. "Now it's time to load the corn into the cart and take it to the miller," said the little red hen. "Who will help?" All together the pig, the duck and the cat replied,

what they were doing while the little hen baked the bread. In a little while a delicious smell came from the kitchen. "The bread is baked," said the little red hen. "Who wants a bite?" "Me, me, me!" cried the pig, the duck and the cat excitedly. "Certainly not," said the little red hen. "You did nothing to help!"

"Not me." They got on with what they were doing while the little hen loaded the cart. The little red hen came back from the mill with a sack of finely ground flour. "It's time to mix the dough to bake the bread," said the little red hen. "Who will help?" Like a choir the pig, the duck and the cat answered, "Not me." They got on with

She and her chicks ate it all and not a crumb was left.

Snow White

Once upon a time there was a wicked queen with a magic mirror. The queen wanted to be the most beautiful woman in the land. But one day, her magic mirror told her, "Snow White is now the most

beautiful." The angry queen ordered a hunter to kill her and bring back her heart. But the hunter took pity on Snow White,

took her deep into the forest and told her to run away. Snow White found the empty cottage of the seven dwarfs, and fell asleep on one of the beds. When the dwarfs got home from work that night they were amazed to find her there. As soon as she opened her eyes, Snow White begged them to let her stay.

faint. When the dwarfs came home, the wicked queen has gone. They could do nothing to bring their friend back to life. With tears in their eyes, they laid her

"The queen wants to kill me and I've nowhere else to go." But the queen's magic mirror told her what had happened. She dressed up as a beggar with a basket of apples and went to the cottage while the dwarfs were at work. Snow White opened the door. One of the apples was poisoned. As soon as Snow White tasted it, she fell to the ground in a deathly

gently in a coffin made of glass. One day, a handsome prince came riding by and saw the glass coffin. Snow White looked so beautiful that he got off his horse and gave her a kiss. At once, Snow White opened here eyes. She had been saved by love!

The Three Little Pigs

Three little pigs decided to build their houses just outside the forest. The first little pig built his house from straw. He finished it very quickly, and went off to

was worried. "Your houses are not strong enough," he told them. "You should use

bricks, like me. If the wolf comes, you will be in trouble." But his brothers just laughed at him and went on playing. A few moments later a big wolf leapt out of the forest. The little pigs ran to their houses.

play. The second little pig built his house from wood. He finished quickly too, and went off to play. But the oldest little pig

The wolf came to the straw house, "Let me in, little pig, or I'll huff and I'll puff and I'll blow your house down." The little pig was scared and did not answer, so the

wolf took a deep breath and huffed and puffed and blew the house down. The little pig ran to his brother's wooden house. Outside the door the wolf roared, "Let me in, little pigs, or I'll huff and I'll puff and I'll blow your house down!" The little

pigs said nothing so the wolf huffed and puffed and blew the house down. The little pigs rushed to their brother's house of bricks. When the wolf came to the little brick house he huffed and he puffed, and he puffed and he huffed, but the house would not fall down. The wolf was very angry, so he climbed onto the roof and slid down the chimney – straight into a pot of boiling water! Howling with pain, the wolf leapt out and raced back into the forest while the three little pigs roared with laughter!

40

The Little Mouse's Wedding

Once upon a time, a most handsome white mouse was born to a family of mice. When he grew up, his parents said, "We shall find the most powerful creature in the universe, and you will marry his daughter." They thought that nothing could be more powerful than the sun,

whose rays warmed the earth.

They asked the sun for his daughter in marriage. "I am honoured," said the sun, "but you are making a mistake. The clouds

are stronger than I am. When I am hidden behind them I can do nothing." The mice looked at the big cloud, full of rain, and thought the sun was right. So they asked the cloud for his daughter.

"I am flattered," replied the cloud, "but you are making a mistake. The wind can push me around the sky as it chooses. It is stronger than I am." The mice thought the cloud was right and went to see the wind to ask for his daughter. "It would be an honour, but you are making a mistake.

I am not as strong as you think. Do you see that wall? However hard I blow, I can never knock it over." The mice looked at the fine stone wall and thought the wind was right. They asked it for its daughter in marriage. "My friends, you are

mistaken," it said. "I am not as strong as you think. The mice that live under me are eating away my foundations, and I will soon fall down. Your son would do better to go and search for a wife among his own kind."